Fawn and the Mysterious Trickster

This edition published by Parragon in 2011
Parragon
Queen Street House
4 Queen Street
Bath BA1 1HE, UK
www.parragon.com

ISBN 978-1-4454-4073-6

Printed in China

Fawn and the Mysterious Trickster

Written by Laura Driscoll
Illustrated by Barbara Nelson
& The Disney Storybook Artists

Bath • New York • Singapore • Hong Kong • Cologne • Delhi
Melbourne • Amsterdam • Johannesburg • Auckland • Shenzhen

Fairies and sparrow men

crowded the Home Tree courtyard.
It was just after dinner on Harvest
Moon Night. The storytelling-talents
were reciting spooky tales. They took
turns trying to outdo one another.

The fairies had already heard
Pip's tale of the giant ladybug. Next
had come Merk's mystery about the
wailing wind. Now it was Tor's turn.

"Isn't this great?" whispered Beck, an animal-talent fairy. She reached for her friend Fawn's arm and squeezed it tightly. Her eyes were wide, and she wore a huge grin.

Fawn nodded. "This is the most scared I've been in a long time!" she whispered gleefully. She wiggled in her seat and tapped her foot on the ground. She couldn't wait to hear what came next!

Tor was just getting to the scariest part of his story. "*Thump, scratch. Thump, scratch.* The mysterious noise grew louder and louder," Tor said. "The fairy backed away from the closed door. It was here, she realized.

She stood frozen to the spot. The doorknob turned! With a long, low creak, the door . . . slowly . . . swung . . . open. Standing there in the shadowy darkness was – "

Pop! Crack! Boom! Three loud noises rang through the courtyard.

All around the circle, fairies jumped in their seats. Bursts of bright red light filled the sky overhead. It had the head of an eagle, it's hooked beak open and screeching. The creature's springy leg and oversized feet looked like a hare's. A long, spiked dragon tail dragged behind it. They formed the image of a hideous creature!

Some fairies gasped. Others cried out. But Fawn grinned. She figured Tor had set it all up. Fawn was a prankster herself, and she knew a good prank when she saw one.

The bursts of red light faded to black. For several breathless moments, no one moved.

Finally, Rani, a water-talent fairy, broke the silence. "Tor, you really scared me!" she cried.

"Me, too!" said Lily, a garden-talent fairy, who was peeking out from behind a toadstool.

"That was the idea!" Tor said, smiling.

Someone giggled. Then a wave of laughter swept around the courtyard.

The stories were over. It was late. Fairies left the courtyard in twos and threes, flying slowly to the Home Tree.

"Tor's story was the spookiest. Don't you think?" Beck asked Fawn.

"Yes!" Fawn agreed. "The prank at the end is what really made it scary!"

Beck nodded as they flew into the Home Tree lobby. "If only Harvest Moon Night came more often," she said with a sigh. Beck yawned a big yawn. "Well, I'm off to bed," she announced. "See you later – I mean, tomorrow."

"Okay, Beck," said Fawn. "Good night."

Fawn flew up to her room. As

she closed the door behind her, she sighed. She was sorry that the spooky storytelling was over.

Maybe I can get Tor to tell another spooky tale tomorrow night, she thought.

She tugged off one boot and dropped it. It hit the floor with a thump.

Maybe he'll let me come up with a prank for the end, she thought.

Fawn dropped the other boot. *Thump.*

She lay back on her bed. It's fun being scared. But it's even more fun to do the scaring! she decided.

Thump. Fawn jumped.

Thump. The noise came again.

It sounded like it was coming from the closet. Fawn flew off her bed. She was halfway to the closet when she heard . . .

Thump, scratch.

Why, that was just like the sound from Tor's story!

Fawn froze. "It's just a noise," she said out loud. "A spooky noise."

Fawn gave herself a little shake. Anything could be making that sound. An animal friend, for instance, like a cricket or a moth. Fawn flew closer to the closet door.

But . . . were her eyes playing tricks on her? Had the doorknob just turned?

The doorknob *was* turning! Fawn
watched it, frozen in horror.

With a long, low creak, the door
slowly swung open.

Standing there in the shadowy darkness was . . .

"Beck!" Fawn cried.

"Boo!" shouted Beck. She flew to Fawn's side. "Did I scare you?" she asked hopefully.

"You scared the pixie dust off me!" Fawn replied. Then it dawned on her. "Wait. You were *trying* to scare me?"

Beck nodded. She flashed a proud

14

smile. "Of course! Tor's story gave
me the idea. So . . ."

Beck laughed. Then she stopped
laughing. She looked worried. "You
aren't . . . angry, are you, Fawn?"
she asked.

"Angry?" Fawn replied, as a smile spread across her face. "No way! That was so great!"

Fawn thought she knew her friend better than anyone. But now Beck had really surprised her. "I didn't know you had it in you, Beck! You definitely got me good!"

Beck beamed. "Really? I wasn't sure I'd be able to prank the pranking queen."

Fawn's glow flared with delight. But she waved off the praise. "Don't be silly," she said. "I couldn't have done it better myself."

Hmm . . . Or could I? she wondered.

Three days later, Fawn woke at first light.

Quickly, she pulled off her pajamas and put on a pair of soft corn-husk ones that looked just like the pajamas Beck wore. Next, she pinned up her long braid. She tucked her dark hair under a corn-husk sleeping cap – just like Beck's. Finally, she grabbed the copper-coloured curtain fringe she had borrowed from the decoration talents. She carefully pinned it to the front of the cap.

Fawn had been planning this for days. She didn't know if she could fool Beck. But if she did, it would be the best prank she'd ever pulled.

Fawn flew to the mirror and studied her reflection. Her disguise wasn't perfect. For one thing, she couldn't make her brown eyes blue, like Beck's. Even so, Fawn was hoping she could fool one very sleepy fairy.

Fawn flew out of her room, zipped down the corridor, and pressed her ear to Beck's door. All was silent. Then, slowly, Fawn pushed the door open and peeked inside.

Beck was still sound asleep. Fawn quietly slipped inside the room, and dove behind her friend's dressing table. Fawn removed the mirror that sat atop the dressing table from its sunflower frame.

Beck tossed, then turned. She

yawned. She propped herself up on one elbow. Then she dragged her feet over the side of the bed. Finally Beck got up and flew sleepily towards her dressing table.

This is it! thought Fawn. She put on her best sleepy face. Beck sat down on her dressing-table chair.

Framed in Beck's sunflower mirror was Fawn – looking just like Beck!

Beck looked into the mirror. Fawn stared sleepily back at her. Beck rubbed her eyes. Fawn rubbed her own. Beck yawned, and so did Fawn.

Now let's see if she's paying attention, thought Fawn. As Beck was about to look away, Fawn winked.

Beck did a double take. She stared at Fawn. Did I just see what I think I saw? her face seemed to say. Fawn made her face say it, too. Beck shook her head, then stretched. Fawn did the same. Beck stared at the mirror warily. Fawn stared back. Beck stretched again, leaning to her right and watching her reflection. Fawn copied her.

Beck leaned closer to the mirror. Fawn leaned forwards, too. Fawn knew she wouldn't be able to fool Beck much longer.

In the blink of an eye, Fawn reached through the mirror frame . . . and tweaked Beck's nose!

"Iiieeee!" Beck screeched.

"What...? Who...? How...?"
Beck stammered. She stared wide-eyed
at the face in her mirror.

Fawn pulled off her disguise. Beck
laughed.

"That was amazing," Beck said. "I
think you've proved who's the best
prankster."

If Fawn hadn't known Beck so well,
she might have missed the twinkle in her

friend's eye. But she knew she hadn't heard the last from Beck!

At first, Fawn was on pins and needles waiting for the next prank. Every time she had a meal in the tearoom, she checked her chair before she sat down. At bedtime, she looked under her pillow before lying down. But days passed, and nothing happened.

One evening, just after dinner, Fawn set out for the dairy barn. She flew very slowly. She was weighed down by the sack of alfalfa seed she had brought as a treat for the mice.

"Anyone here?" Fawn squeaked in Mouse language as she flew into the barn.

The dairy mice squeaked a greeting back. Fawn was quickly surrounded by her four-legged friends.

She passed out the alfalfa seed and gossiped with the mice as they snacked.

Fawn had been talking for quite a while when she saw two shadows – a mouse's and her own – on the wall of the barn. She hadn't noticed them before. But she shrugged it off and went back to chatting.

But then a movement on the wall caught her eye. She glanced over. It wasn't a mouse shadow. Whatever or whoever it belonged to had a giant head!

As Fawn watched, the shadow raised two enormous arms. Its long fingers were outstretched like claws! Whatever it was, it was right behind her!

Fawn wheeled around. But she didn't see a monster. She couldn't see anything! A blinding light shone in her eyes.

All of a sudden, the bright light dimmed. Fawn blinked several times.

There was Beck with her wings tucked in. She had been playing the part of the giant shadow monster. Behind her was Fira, a light-talent fairy. They were both giggling.

Fawn groaned. "Beck! You got me

again!" She felt like kicking herself for being fooled. She had been ready – and she'd gotten tricked anyway!

Still, Fawn congratulated Beck and Fira on their fine – and frightening – prank.

But Fawn wasn't about to be outdone.

Over the next few days, the pranks came fast and furious. Fawn replaced Beck's shampoo with maple syrup. Beck's hair stood straight up for two days and through five washings! Beck sprinkled fairy dust onto Fawn's breakfast roll so that it floated away before Fawn could eat it. Fawn replaced Beck's favourite clothes with bigger and bigger sizes to make her think she was shrinking.

One night, Beck stuffed two dozen maple seedpods into Fawn's closet. They rained down on Fawn when she went to get dressed the next morning.

As she stood ankle-deep in seedpods, Fawn couldn't help admiring Beck's creativity. "Pretty good, Beck," she said. "But you haven't seen my best pranks yet!"

All day long, Fawn plotted and schemed.

Fawn was still plotting at bedtime. She wanted her next prank to be a really good one. But nothing was coming to her!

She drifted off to sleep, still thinking about pranks.

That night, Fawn dreamed that she and Beck were on a beach. They stood side by side at the water's edge. Beck filled an acorn cup with seawater. She emptied it into a shell bucket at Fawn's feet. Beck turned to fill the cup again. When Beck wasn't looking, Fawn dumped the bucket out onto the sand. She put it down before Beck turned around. Beck refilled the bucket. Fawn dumped it out again. Beck kept filling it. Fawn kept secretly emptying it – turning the bucket over, over, over.

Fawn awoke to sunlight on her pillow. Bits of the dream were still floating around in her mind.

"Wow!" she said to herself. "I'm even pranking in my sleep!"

Fawn's bedroom door burst open. There stood Beck, hands planted on her hips.

"Okay," she said. "I have *no* idea how you did it – and without waking me up!"

"Huh?" Fawn said, sitting up in bed.

"When did you do it?" Beck went on. "Last night after I went to sleep?" She flew to Fawn's bed and plopped down next to her. "Or did you get up early this morning? When I woke up and looked around, I couldn't figure out what was going on. With everything upside down, I felt like I was upside down!" Beck laughed.

"What?" Fawn cried. She hopped out of bed and pulled on her tunic and pumpkin-coloured leggings. She had to see what Beck was talking about. She flew out of the room ahead of Beck. She was hovering in the open doorway of Beck's room, her eyes wide, when her friend caught up.

It was the oddest sight. Every picture and wall hanging was upside down. Every bottle and knickknack

the dressing table was stood on its head.
Beck's firefly lanterns, her chestnut
water pitcher and cup, even some of her
small furniture – all of it was turned
wrong way up.

Fawn darted around the room,
getting a closer look. "Wow!" she said at
last.

"When I finally did figure it out, I
couldn't stop laughing," Beck said. "It's
hilarious!"

Fawn giggled. "It is funny," she agreed.
"I only wish I had thought of it!"

Beck did a double take. "What?"

"I didn't do it!" Fawn insisted.
"Really!"

Beck's brow wrinkled. She looked

around her room. "But Fawn," she said, "if you didn't do it . . ."

"Who did?" Fawn finished.

Fawn and Beck were still puzzling over the mystery as they flew down to the tearoom.

"I bet it was a friend of ours," Beck was saying. "Someone who knows what we've been up to."

The two fairies found seats together at the animal-talent table. Fawn was reaching for a slice of lemon poppy-seed cake when Tinker Bell flew by.

"Fawn, Beck," Tink called. "What's new with the pranking?"

"Why do you ask?" Fawn replied. She fixed Tink with a questioning stare.

But Tink just gave them a little wave and flew on to the pots-and-pans-talent table.

"Now, Tink . . ." Fawn said to Beck. "She's not one to shy away from mischief. She might have done it!"

Fawn and Beck had a delicious breakfast of lemon poppy-seed cake and fresh-squeezed berry juice, but Fawn couldn't stop thinking about who had pranked Beck.

As they were leaving the tearoom, Fira flew in. She winked at Fawn as she passed by her and Beck.

Fawn stopped in midair and turned. "Wait!" she called after Fira.

"What?" Fira said, flying backwards.

"You winked at me!" Fawn said. "Why?"

Fira gave Fawn a funny look. "Well, you know. The prank the other day. In the barn. I helped Beck trick you," she reminded Fawn. "I hope there are no hard feelings."

Fawn studied Fira's face carefully. "Is that all?"

Fira nodded. "What else would there be?" she asked. She shrugged and then flew off.

Fawn turned to Beck. "I've got it!" she exclaimed. "Fira had fun pranking me. So she decided to prank you, too! You know, just to be fair!"

Beck looked doubtful. "But she

really didn't seem to know anything about it."

Fawn had to admit Beck was right. Fira was probably innocent.

For the rest of the day, the two fairies were on the lookout for suspects.

That evening in Fawn's room, Fawn and Beck wrote down all their suspects on a leaf. It was a long list.

Beck let out a big sigh. "I guess we aren't any closer to figuring out who our mystery prankster is," she said.

They were both silent. The wind picked up outside the Home Tree. It whistled eerily through the hollow spaces of the great old maple. Suddenly, Fawn stopped and stared at Beck. Her eyes widened.

"What if our prankster isn't a fairy?" she said.

"What do you mean?" Beck asked.

"Maybe it's not a fairy! Not a sparrow man!" Fawn cried. She landed next to Beck. "What if our prankster is . . . a ghost?"

The next morning, Fawn woke up and threw her legs over the side of her bed. Just like every morning, she felt around for her slippers with her feet. And just like every morning, she found the slippers lined up neatly next to her bed.

But this morning, unlike every morning, her feet came down on the slippers with a squishy splat.

Fawn looked down. Her slippers were covered with some kind of shiny green goo!

"Eewwww!" Fawn cried, wincing. Then she looked at her feet more closely. "What in Never Land is this stuff?" She glanced around for something to wipe her feet with. That was when she noticed: there was green goo all over her mirror!

Fawn flew out of bed. Her dresser was covered in goo, too. Her toadstool night table, the foot of her bed – lots of things were splattered or smeared with it. Globs of green goo dotted her floor. They seemed to form a little trail leading towards the door.

As Fawn was getting dressed, someone knocked on her door. Beck rushed in.

"I've been slimed!" she cried. Then she noticed Fawn's mirror. "Oh! You've been slimed, too! Come look at my room."

Fawn followed Beck down the corridor. Sure enough, when they reached Beck's room, Fawn saw a slimy mess.

Beck studied a glob of slime on her doorknob. "What is it?"

"I don't know," said Fawn. More slime on the floor outside Beck's door caught her eye. "But there's some out here!" Fawn zipped farther

down the corridor. "And over here! And down there, too!" She looked back at Beck. "Let's see where it leads!" Fawn cried.

With Beck right behind her, Fawn followed the trail of slime. It ran down the stairs to the lobby and then into the tearoom.

Some fairies were already there having breakfast. Fawn and Beck wove around the tables. No one else seemed to notice the slime. It blended in well with the tearoom's fresh flower carpet. But Fawn and Beck knew what they were looking for.

They kept their eyes on the trail. It led them through the swinging door of the kitchen. Inside, the kitchen-talents were busy preparing breakfast. Fawn and Beck zigged and zagged around them – one eye on the kitchen traffic and one on the slime.

Then, in the pantry, the trail ended. Fawn and Beck looked all around. But there was no more slime to be seen.

"That's it?" said Beck, looking down. "That's the end?"

"I don't think so," Fawn replied. "I think this is the end." She pointed to the cupboard in front of them. "I'll bet that whatever made the slime is inside this cupboard."

Beck drew back. Fawn held her

breath. She flung open the cupboard doors. But all she found were jars, tins and canisters.

"Wait!" Fawn cried. She picked up a jar from one of the shelves. It was missing its lid and a teaspoon was sticking out of it. Fawn examined the jar more closely. "It's filled with slime! No, not slime. It's . . ."

"What? What?" Beck cried.

Fawn scooped up some slime with her finger. Then, with a wink at Beck, she ate it!

Beck stared wide-eyed at Fawn. "What are you doing?"

Fawn just smiled.

Beck looked at the jar label. Her

jaw dropped. "Kiwifruit jam?" she exclaimed in disbelief.

Fawn started to laugh. She laughed so hard she snorted. "Someone really got us, Beck," she said.

Before long, Beck was doubled over laughing too. A couple of kitchen talents peeked into the pantry. They threw Fawn and Beck questioning looks, but the two fairies were laughing too hard to explain anything.

It took Fawn and Beck

hours to clean up all the green jam.
By the time they were getting ready
for bed, Fawn still felt sticky between
her toes.

Beck was settling into a little bed
she and Fawn had made in Fawn's
room. She hadn't wanted to sleep
alone in her room, not after two nights
in a row of unexplained mischief.

"We'll have a sleepover!" Fawn had suggested that afternoon. "Maybe we'll set a trap for our mystery prankster!"

They had tacked a superfine spiderweb across Fawn's doorway. Then they had tied a row of bells along its edges.

They had set up another, similar trap across Fawn's open window.

As she snuggled in for the night, Fawn felt confident. "No one is getting in here without us knowing about it," she said.

"No fairy, you mean," Beck replied. Fawn could hear the smile in her voice. "Ghosts can float right through spiderwebbing."

Fawn giggled. "Sleep well, Beck."

"Sleep well, Fawn," Beck replied.

As she tried to fall asleep, Fawn replayed the events of the day in her mind. Then she noticed a soft sound. It was Beck breathing, sound asleep. Fawn found herself breathing in the same rhythm – in, out, in, out, in . . . Soon, she was fast asleep too.

The next thing Fawn knew, a strange sound startled her awake.

"Fawn, did you hear that?" asked Beck. She was sitting up on her pile of cushions.

"I heard something," Fawn replied. "What was it?"

There it was again. It was a creepy wail. Beck looked at Fawn with wide eyes.

"That was it," she said.

As animal talents, Fawn and Beck had heard plenty of strange noises. But this noise was different. This was eerie and unnatural. It was like a sound from another world.

"Come on! We've got to find out what's making it," Fawn said. She leaped out of bed. "Where is it coming from, anyway?" Without thinking, she flung open the door and stuck her head out to listen.

"Fawn, wait!" Beck cried.

But it was too late.

BRRRRRRRRRIIIIIIIIIIINNNG!

Fawn's head got caught in the trap.

All the tiny bells began to ring loudly.

"Aaaah!" Fawn cried in alarm.

Beck cringed and covered her ears.

The spiderweb stuck to Fawn's

head and shoulders. As she struggled

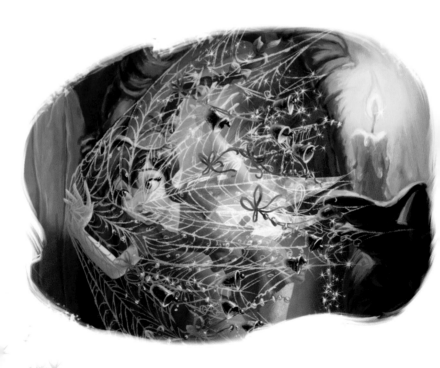

to get it off, the bells continued to ring. Finally, with Beck's help, Fawn removed the web. She dropped it on the floor.

"Now we know the trap works!" said Fawn. Her heart was pounding.

They heard the wail again. "It's coming from outside the window," Fawn said. "But that's booby-trapped, too." She led the way into the corridor. "We'll go this way instead!"

Together, Beck and Fawn flew down to the lobby. At the front door, they stopped, and slowly stuck their heads outside. They peered out at blackness. It was a cloudy night. No moon, no stars – nothing to see by.

Even so, Fawn flew out into it. Beck followed.

"Beck! Look!" Fawn whispered. "Over there!" She pointed to a spot on a branch of the Home Tree. As they stared, something moved ever so slightly. There was a faint rustling of leaves. A moment later, they heard the wail again.

Beck pointed just beyond the end of the branch. "Isn't that your window, Fawn?" she asked.

Fawn nodded. "Whatever it is, it's sitting right outside my room!"

Just then, a dark shape darted from the leaves.

Fawn thought it was about the size

of a fairy, but she didn't see any wings. And yet it could fly! While Fawn watched, it moved to one side and hovered there, motionless.

It let out a piercing wail that made Fawn's hair stand on end.

"What is it?" Beck whispered in Fawn's ear.

"I don't know," Fawn whispered back. "But I do know one thing."

"What?" said Beck.

Fawn swallowed hard. "That's no fairy."

The mysterious shape

disappeared behind another cluster of leaves.

"Let's get a closer look!" Fawn whispered.

They inched forwards, moving as quietly as they could.

Before they could reach the spot, the shape darted away. It landed on a nearby branch. Again, Fawn and Beck inched towards it. And again, it darted to a branch just as they got close.

On the third try, they closed in. They paused in front of the leaves shielding the mystery wailer. Fawn reached out and grasped a leaf stem. Slowly, slowly, she pulled the curtain of leaves aside.

A small, feathered head with a long, thin beak poked out at them.

"Twitter?" Beck cried in surprise.

Fawn couldn't believe that the little bird was the source of that awful wail.

Twitter and Beck had been close
since Twitter was a chick. As long as
Beck had known him, Twitter had
always been a little high-strung. He
tended to get overexcited about the
smallest things. When he did, he often
came looking for Beck.

"Twitter," said Beck in Hummingbird, "what are you doing up at this

time of night? And why are you making that awful noise? Are you all right?"

Fawn couldn't help eyeing Twitter suspiciously.

"Wait!" Fawn cried in Hummingbird. "I've got it now. You're the mystery prankster!"

Beck looked shocked. Twitter himself looked positively bewildered. "What p-p-prankster? N-n-no!" He flitted around excitedly. "I j-j-just have a little c-c-cold," Twitter stuttered. "I couldn't sleep. I just d-d-didn't know what to do with myself. So I came out here to p-p-practise my new hummingbird song. Like this."

Twitter tipped his head back. Out came the noise that had woken Fawn and Beck up. Only now it didn't sound much like a wail. It sounded like a hummingbird with a cold trying to sing.

"Aaaaaaaaooooooooooooeeeeeeeee!" Twitter moaned.

Fawn's and Beck's eyes met. They couldn't help smiling. To think they had mistaken a singing bird for a wailing ghost!

The fairies flew Twitter back to his nest and tucked him in. Then they laughed over their silliness all the way back to the Home Tree.

By the time they flew back into

Fawn's room, they could barely keep their eyes open.

Fawn fell into her bed. There was nothing standing between her and sleep.

"*Ieee!*"

Fawn rolled over. Her eyelids felt heavy. She struggled to get them open. But what she saw woke her up fast.

Dulcie, a baking-talent fairy, was looking down at Fawn, her eyes wide and her mouth open in surprise.

"Aaaah!" Fawn cried, startled.

Fawn looked over Dulcie's head. That's funny, she thought. Who

moved that pot rack from the kitchen to my room?

Fawn sat bolt upright. She was in the kitchen. She looked down. She'd been lying on a table.

Fawn knew she had fallen asleep in her bedroom. So how had she wound up in the kitchen? There seemed to be only one explanation.

The mystery prankster had moved her while she slept!

Dulcie was still trembling a
little as she told Fawn how she had
found her.

"I was going to get all my ingredients
from the pantry," Dulcie told Fawn.
"I came over to put them on this table.
You were completely covered by the
tablecloth." Dulcie held up Fawn's
'blanket'. "I had no idea you were
there until I moved it."

"But I don't understand," Dulcie went on. "You say someone moved you from your bed? While you slept? As a joke?" She crossed her arms. "It doesn't seem very funny to me."

Fawn put an arm around Dulcie. "Really? Because I think it's hilarious!" She told Dulcie about the other pranks she and Beck had been dealing with.

Dulcie giggled. "That is kind of funny. But who do you think is behind it?" she asked.

"I have no idea!" Fawn exclaimed in frustration.

After she left the kitchen, Fawn raced upstairs to wake Beck. She had to tell her what had happened!

Fawn flew past her own door
on her way to Beck's before she
remembered – Beck was sleeping in
her room. Fawn backtracked and
burst through the door.

"Beck! Beck!" she cried. "You've got
to hear this!" Fawn lifted the sheet that
Beck had pulled over her face while she
slept.

"Huh?" Beck grunted sleepily. But she woke up in a hurry when Fawn launched into her tale.

"How did someone move you down to the kitchen without waking you up?" Beck asked in disbelief after Fawn had finished.

"Well," Fawn said, "I *am* a very sound sleeper."

Beck frowned. "But . . . how did the prankster even get in here?" she asked. "The place was booby-trapped."

Fawn shook her head. "Not quite. Remember, we tripped the trap on the door last night?"

"Oh, right," Beck said. "When we

came back to bed, we didn't set it up again."

"I guess the prankster came right in through the door," said Fawn.

Fawn flew slowly across the room while staring at the floor. Then she turned and flew slowly back. Beck watched her. After crossing the room a dozen times, Fawn stopped.

"Okay. I say we go all out," Fawn said. "Tonight. We set up booby traps again, only this time we set up more! And not just here, but all over the Home Tree!"

Beck gave Fawn a doubtful look.

"You're right, you're right." Fawn sighed. "That's a little crazy. Okay.

How about this – we set a couple of traps in each of the main corridors. That's bound to catch anyone who's flying around and up to no good."

"Let's do it," Beck said. "There's just one thing. What if we catch someone who's not the prankster?"

Fawn waved the question away. "We can worry about that when we catch someone!"

Getting the trap ready took most of the day. Fawn got rolls and rolls of spiderweb from the weaving talents.

She was already unrolling the webs in her room when Beck came in with the bells. As they tied the bells to the webs, they worked out a plan. They

would wait to set up the traps until everyone was asleep. Otherwise, fairies would be tripping the traps left and right.

"And this time, I'm not going to sleep," said Fawn. "I want to stay alert – no mistakes like last time."

9

"Do you see anyone?" Beck whispered.

"No, no not yet," Fawn whispered back.

The two fairies were squashed into a tiny space behind a plant stand in the hallway.

Beck peeked out from behind one side of the plant stand. Fawn peeked out the other side. By the faint light of the firefly lanterns on the wall, Beck could see the door of her room. And Fawn could see the door of her room. Together, they could keep an eye on both corridors that led to their hiding place.

They had set two traps. Fawn squinted, trying to make out the traps in her corridor. But it was too dark to see any of the superfine webs.

"Do you see anyone now?" Beck whispered.

"No," Fawn whispered. "No one."

Time inched by. Fawn stared down the corridor. She studied every detail. She heard the trees outside rustle in the wind. A cold breeze blew down the corridor. Fawn shivered.

Crrrrrreeeeeeeeeak. The two fairies jumped at the noise.

They were both silent for several moments, listening. Then Beck whispered, "Fawn, what if . . . what if we don't catch anyone and we're still pranked?"

"What?" Fawn whispered. "You mean, what if someone gets by all our traps? Then I guess . . . that would *prove* that our prankster is . . . a ghost."

Out of the corner of her eye, Fawn saw something. A stone's throw away, a small, dark shape moved across the floor. It was coming towards Fawn!

"Aaaah!" Fawn cried.

"What?" Beck said, turning to see.

Fawn stammered, "It's a . . . a . . ."

The dark shape skittered away down the corridor. Fawn exhaled. It was just a beetle passing through the Home Tree.

Fawn took some deep breaths. She

leaned her head against the plant stand. Behind her, Beck started humming very softly.

Fawn listened to Beck's song, 'Fairy Dust Melody'. The music talents had played it at the last Full Moon Dance.

Fawn closed her eyes just for a second. She could see the courtyard as it had looked the night of the twilight dance. The light-talent fairies had made lovely coloured lanterns. The decoration talents had hung ribbon streamers from the low branches. The cooking and baking talents had filled tables with special treats. And once the dance was in full swing, all the different colours of the fairies' dresses mingled together, as they swirled around and around and around. . . .

Just then, a loud ringing filled the hallway.

BRRRRRRRRRIIIIIIIIIIINNNG!

The trap!

Fawn's eyes snapped open. She scanned the dark corridor. "Who is it?" she cried. "Where are they? Beck? Beck?"

Beck was standing nearby. She stared at Fawn with wide eyes.

"Beck, why are you just standing there? The trap! It's been tripped!" said Fawn.

Beck said nothing. She opened her

mouth to speak, then closed it again. She raised an arm slowly and pointed.

Fawn looked down. Wrapped all around her body were superfine spiderwebs tied with bells. Only then did she also notice that she wasn't crouched behind the plant stand. She was standing in the middle of the hallway. How had she gotten there? She had no memory of moving.

"Beck, I don't understand," Fawn said. "What's going on? Where's the mystery trickster?"

"Fawn," Beck said breathlessly, "the trickster is . . . you!"

Fawn was trying to become airborne, but the spiderwebs kept her wings from moving freely. "Could you give me a hand with this?"

Beck stretched the sticky webs so that Fawn could wriggle out of them. "You are the mystery trickster!" Beck said.

Fawn couldn't believe what she was hearing. "That's ridiculous!" she replied. "Wouldn't I know if I were?"

Beck shook her head. "Not if you were sleeping."

Fawn stopped wriggling. "Sleeping?" she cried. "Sleeping while I turned your room upside down? Sleeping while I spread jam all over the Home Tree? Sleeping while I went downstairs to nap on the kitchen table?"

Beck nodded. "I just watched you dance in your sleep," Beck said. "You danced right into that booby trap. You got up from behind the plant stand. I asked what you were doing. But you didn't answer. Then you started twirling around the hallway." Beck closed her eyes and demonstrated.

"I called your name over and over. Your eyes were shut and you didn't seem to hear me. Before I knew it, you had danced right into the trap. And when the bells went off . . . you woke up." Beck stopped dancing and shrugged. "Fawn, I think you were sleep flying!"

Fawn was quiet. She wanted to laugh it off. But a voice inside was telling her that Beck was on to something.

Fawn thought back to the night Beck's room was turned upside down. "I had a dream the night of the first mystery prank," Fawn recalled. "I was turning a bucket of water over, again and again."

Beck thought about that. "Maybe you were acting that out in my room?" she suggested. "Did you have a dream the night of the jam prank?"

Fawn shook her head. "I don't remember one. But I do love kiwifruit jam," she said. "Maybe I was hungry for a midnight snack!"

Beck held up a finger. "And maybe you were going back for more the night you wound up on the kitchen table!"

Fawn shrugged. The sleep-flying prankster theory was starting to add up.

"I think you might be right, Beck!" Fawn exclaimed. "I am the mystery prankster!" A huge grin spread across her face. "And I'm such a good prank-ster, I can do it in my sleep!"

Fawn still had trouble believing it. But she knew it had to be true. She and Beck had gotten so carried away with their pranking that it had taken over every part of their lives – even Fawn's sleep.

Suddenly, Fawn felt very tired. She yawned a huge yawn. She hadn't been sleeping well lately, and now she knew why.

As Fawn went back to her own bed, she made a decision. She would set up a booby trap in her door and one in her window every night before she went to bed. It would make her feel better. She didn't really want to be pranking other fairies in her sleep.

The next morning, Fawn waved cheerfully at Beck as she flew into the tearoom for breakfast. "Fly with you, Beck!" Fawn said.

"Fly with you, Fawn!" replied Beck. She took the seat next to Fawn and reached for a platter of pancakes. "Up to any more midnight mystery pranks last night?" Beck asked.

"Not that I can remember!" Fawn replied.

Beck picked up the jug of blueberry syrup next to her plate. She poured some onto her pancakes. Then she put the jug back in the centre of the table.

She let go of the jug, but it wouldn't let go of her. It was stuck to her hand! Beck shook and shook her hand, but she couldn't shake the jug free!

Beck looked at Fawn sideways.

"Okay," Fawn said, "that one I do remember."

Join the Disney Fairies on their next Pixie Hollow adventure...

Iridessa, Lost at Sea

Iridessa snapped her fingers, and sparks flew from her fingertips. The sparks twinkled briefly before they were snuffed out.

Iridessa was a light-talent fairy, and she was practicing for the Full Moon Dance.

The next full moon was still many nights away. Most light-talent fairies hadn't even begun practicing yet. But

Iridessa wanted to be absolutely perfect.

Iridessa spun through the air and then turned to watch the trail of sparkles fade into the darkness behind her. Three sparkles had escaped and were not in the right order. Many fairies wouldn't have noticed, but Iridessa did. She sighed. "Not quite perfect," she muttered. "Yet."

Suddenly, Iridessa heard a flutter and a low hoot. Something with large wings flapped overhead.

Iridessa dove into a nearby bush for shelter.

An owl landed next to the bush. She saw a round, yellow eye peering in at her.

Iridessa held her breath.

The owl hooted again and then pecked at the bush with its sharp, curved beak. He kept his fierce yellow eyes trained on Iridessa. She was trapped!

Suddenly, she had an idea. She snapped her fingers, sending out a streak of blinding light. The owl hopped backwards, surprised. He blinked twice, then flew away.

Iridessa stayed in the bush for several minutes. Finally, she poked her head out. There was no sign of the owl. Iridessa flew to the Home Tree as fast as she could.

"All-fairy meeting!" Iridessa shouted, as she flew down the hallway. "In the courtyard! Right away!"

Iridessa flew through each branch of the Home Tree, banging on doors and sounding the alarm. By the time she reached the courtyard, it was packed with sleepy fairies and sparrow men.

"What's going on?" someone called to her. "Why did you drag us out of bed?"

"I was just attacked by an owl!" Iridessa announced.

The fairies gasped.

Beck, an animal-talent fairy, flew

over and landed next to Iridessa.

"Fawn and I found the owl's nest not ten frog leaps from the Home Tree. It wouldn't talk to us. The owl was completely wild."

"Ten frog leaps is too close," said a sparrow man named Chirp.

"So what are we going to do?" Tink asked.

Just then, Queen Clarion flew into the courtyard. She looked around at the frightened fairies and sparrow men. "It seems we have a very serious problem," she said.

"We do, Your Majesty," Iridessa agreed.

"We must find a way to make the

owl move. What we need in this situation," the queen said, "is an organized fairy. Someone brave and clever enough to think of a way to make the owl go away."

Maybe someone like Fira, Iridessa thought. She's brave and clever. Or Rani, although she isn't very organized.

"It seems to me that you, Iridessa, are the perfect fairy for the job," the queen finished.

"Good idea!" Beck said. "Iridessa is the smartest, most organized fairy in Pixie Hollow!"

Iridessa was about to protest. But she looked out at the crowd of fairies and saw their eager, hopeful faces. Then she glanced at Queen Clarion. The queen was smiling at her. Iridessa swallowed hard.

"All right," Iridessa agreed. "I'll think of something."

Other titles in this series:

Beck and the
Great Berry Battle

Iridessa, Lost at Sea

Lily's Pesky Plant

Silvermist and the
Ladybird Curse

The Trouble with Tink

Tink, North of Never Land

Vidia and the Fairy Crown